Bjørnstjerne Bjørnson

Pastor Sang

Being the Norwegian drama over aevne

Bjørnstjerne Bjørnson

Pastor Sang
Being the Norwegian drama over aevne

ISBN/EAN: 9783337394530

Printed in Europe, USA, Canada, Australia, Japan

Cover: Foto ©Andreas Hilbeck / pixelio.de

More available books at **www.hansebooks.com**

PASTOR SANG

BEING THE

NORWEGIAN DRAMA

OVER ÆVNE

BY

BJÖRNSTJERNE BJÖRNSON

TRANSLATED INTO ENGLISH,

FOR THE AUTHOR, BY

WILLIAM WILSON

LONDON

LONGMANS, GREEN AND CO.

AND NEW YORK: 15 EAST 16TH ST.

1893

The words 'Over Ævne' mean literally 'over power.' They suggest the striving for something beyond the striver's strength, and his consequent state. This state might be suggested by such an epithet as 'exalté,' or 'overwrought,' or 'überspannt.'

DRAMATIS PERSONÆ

ADOLPH SANG, a pastor.

KLARA SANG, his wife.

ELIAS, their son.

RAKEL, their daughter.

Mrs. ROBERTS (HANNA), Fru Sang's sister.

THE BISHOP.

KRÖJER.

A STRANGER (BRANT).

BLANK.

BREJ. } Pastors.

FALK.

JENSEN.

A PASTOR'S WIDOW.

AAGAAT FLORVAAGEN.

Other clergymen, a crowd of people.

Scene.—A scattered hamlet, on a fjord in the extreme north of Norway.

The orthography of the original Norse indicates that two of the pastors, Blank and Brej, pronounce their words in a pedantic and rather affected way. For instance, the words *Gud vor Fader* are written *Goud vor Fäder*. Phonetic equivalents exist in English, but they are unsuited to the characters, and would disfigure the page.

OVER ÆVNE

THE FIRST ACT

A plain room with timber walls. In the right hand wall are two 'croisées' windows opening above and below; in the left a door.

A bed stands in front, more to the right hand than to the left, and so placed that the head is in a line with the door.

By the bed is a little table with bottles and cups upon it. There are a chest of drawers, chairs, and other furniture.

THE FIRST SCENE

In the bed, covered with a white counterpane, lies KLARA (*Fru Sang*), *clad in white. At one of the windows stands her sister,* HANNA (*Mrs. Roberts*).

HANNA

How the sun shines on the birch leaves!
——And how delicate the foliage is here!

A

KLARA

Yes, but now there is a smell of cherry blossom !

HANNA

I am looking everywhere for it ; but there is no cherry blossom.

KLARA

You cannot see it from where you are ; but there is some.   The morning breeze brings the scent right upon us.

HANNA

I cannot smell it.

KLARA

Ah, after rain like this I can smell the least breath of scent from the open air.

HANNA

And you can smell cherry blossom ?

KLARA

Quite distinctly !——At any rate shut the lower window.

HANNA

Certainly, if you like.   [*She does so.*

KLARA

Who was it that said there was reason to fear a landslip from the mountain ?

HANNA

The old man, who manages the boat that fetched us. It kept on raining and raining, and then he said : ‘ This is dangerous. After such a continuance of rain the fells get loosened.’

KLARA

I have thought of nothing else all night. There has been landslip after landslip here, you know. Once——but that was before our time——the church was carried away.

HANNA

The church !

KLARA

Not from where the present church stands. It stood further off then.

HANNA

Is that why it was moved so close up to the garden wall ?

KLARA

Yes. Now, in the summer, when the church windows are taken out, I can lie and hear Adolf singing at the altar. That is to say, this door has to be open and the door into the sitting-room,——and of course the window of the sitting-room is open too. He sings so beautifully. When both the doors are open, I can see the church from where I lie. Come here! That is why the bed is placed so.

HANNA

[*Going to her.*] Dear Klara, to think that I should come to find you like this.

KLARA

Hanna!

HANNA

Why did you not write to me?

KLARA

In the first place, America is so far off, you know; and in the second——Well!——in the second——another time for that——

HANNA

I did not understand your answer yesterday, when I asked about the doctor.

KLARA

Adolf was here, so I evaded the question. We do not have a doctor.

HANNA

You do not have any doctor?

KLARA

He kept on coming and coming——the

doctor lives a very long way off——and nothing came of it. And when I had lain like that for a whole month without sleeping . .

HANNA

A whole month without sleeping? But that is quite impossible. . . . !

KLARA

Now it is nearly six weeks!——Well you see the doctor could not have been making any difference, could he? My husband asked him what was the matter with me, and he gave the illness an ugly name. Adolf did not tell me, so I do not know what it was. Since then we have not sent for him.

HANNA

Are you not talking too much?

KLARA

For whole days I do not speak at all. At other times I talk incessantly. I cannot help it.

Adolf will be coming back directly from his morning walk, and then he will have some flowers for me.

HANNA

Cannot I pick you some, if you long for them so?

KLARA

No. There are certain kinds that I cannot
endure. He knows which.

Hanna, you have not told me about your
meeting with my children on the steamer. I
am frightfully anxious to hear about it.

HANNA

There was such a confusion here yesterday.

KLARA

And you were all so tired. Fancy, the
children are asleep still! From seven o'clock
until seven! That is youth!

HANNA

And they need it too. While I can only
sleep a few hours at a time. And even then
I am not tired.

KLARA

No, every one is like that, who comes up
under the midnight sun. One is so flooded
with wakefulness.——But the children? Are
not they sweet?

HANNA

They are, and they are so innocent! But
they are not like you in the face, nor Sang
either exactly, except the eyes; I saw that,
afterwards.

KLARA

Go on! Go on!

HANNA

If they had been like you, I should certainly have recognised them.——I have not seen either of you since you were young yourselves. Think of that!——I saw them come on board, and I saw them again afterwards, though they travelled second class. . . .

KLARA

——They could not afford more, poor dears!

HANNA

——and I never recognised them. Then one morning, I was standing on the bridge of the steamer, and they were walking quickly to and fro beneath me, trying to keep warm. Every time they turned their backs to me, to go up the deck again, I could not forget their eyes. I knew the eyes. Then some sea-birds swooped down so close to them, that Rakel was frightened, and struck at them with her arms, for they shrieked almost into her ear. But that movement of the arms,——that was like you exactly. And then I recognised the eyes too! They were Sang's.

KLARA

You went down to them at once?

HANNA

Can you ask! 'Is your name Sang?' I
asked. They had no need to answer. I saw
then plainly enough. 'I am Aunt Hanna from
America,' I said.——And then we were all so
much moved.   [*Both the sisters cry.*

KLARA

Rakel had written to you and asked you
to make the journey over here to see me?
Was not that so?

HANNA

Yes. And I shall never cease to thank
Rakel for it. She was so sweet! I got them
over at once into the first-class cabin and
wrapped her in a large shawl, for she was
freezing. He got a plaid over him.

KLARA

Dear Hanna!

HANNA

But, Klara,——yes, this is part of the story!
——just then a black wind blew up the fjord
behind us. We were right under a high, bare,
grey fell. A flock of seamews flew out; a pair
of them shrieked over our heads. It *was* so
cold. Some poor cottages on the beach!——
and they were the only ones we could see, and
we had travelled many miles without seeing

any others. Nothing but rock and skerry!
'This is the Norlands,' I thought. 'This is where
these poor frozen children have been reared.'
No, I shall never forget it! It is frightful.

KLARA

But it is not frightful.

HANNA

Klara!——To think of you lying there?
Do you remember what an active, graceful
creature you were?

KLARA

Yes, yes!——I do not know either, how I
could begin to explain it all to you. O God!

HANNA

Why did you not cry out to me, when I
am so well off? There are so many ways in
which I could have saved you from being
overstrained?
Why did you not write the truth? You
have concealed it the whole time.——Rakel
was the first to write truth.

KLARA

Yes, yes !——That is so,——and must have
been so.

HANNA

Why? .

KLARA

Supposing I had written how things were, and you had all come rushing over together . . .?

I will not be helped. For I cannot be helped.

HANNA

And so you wrote what was not true?——

KLARA

Yes, and naturally too. I lied continually . . . to every one. How could I do otherwise?

HANNA

It is all quite unintelligible! From beginning to end.

KLARA

Hanna? You said 'overstrained.' You said you could have saved me in many ways from being overstrained. Have you ever known any one overstrained who could ask for help? or who understood how to offer any resistance?

HANNA

But before you had become overstrained?

KLARA

You do not understand what you are talking about!

HANNA

Then explain it to me,——if you can.

KLARA

No, I cannot all at once.——But gradually
I may perhaps.

HANNA

Then, to begin with, you did not hold his
faith?——So extraordinary!——Was that the
cause?

KLARA

No.——Ah, it is a long story!——But it is
not *that*. We have such different natures;——
although it is not that either. If Sang had
been like other men, and blustered and made
a noise, then there would have been no
danger,——perhaps! But long before he knew
me, all his energy——and believe me, he has
energy!——was absorbed in his work; it had
passed into love, into self-sacrifice. It was
simply and entirely beautiful! Do you know,
that no hard word has ever yet been heard in
our house? There has never been a 'scene.'
And we shall soon have been married for
twenty-five years. His face is always lit
with the joy of Sunday. For with him the
Lord's day lasts throughout the year.

HANNA

Good God! how you do love him!

KLARA

To say that I love him is too little, I do not exist without him. And yet you talk of offering resistance? —— At least, —— I was forced to do so, sometimes, when it went too far beyond every one's power.

HANNA

What do you mean by that?

KLARA

I will explain that to you later. But who can resist pure, simple goodness? pure, simple self-sacrifice for others, pure, simple joy? And who can resist, when his childlike faith and his supernatural power carry every one else away with them?

HANNA

Supernatural, did you say?

KLARA

Have not you heard? Did not the children tell you—— ?

HANNA

What?

KLARA

—— that when Sang prays from his heart, he obtains what he prays for?

HANNA

Do you mean, that he works miracles?

KLARA

Yes!

HANNA

Sang?!

KLARA

Did not the children tell you?

HANNA

No!

KLARA

But that is extraordinary!

HANNA

We did not talk at all about that kind of thing.

KLARA

Then they could not have . . . Ah! they thought you knew it! For Sang is 'the miracle pastor' all over the country! They thought you knew about it! They are so modest, those children.

HANNA

But does he work miracles?——Miracles?

KLARA

Did you not receive an impression, directly you saw him, of something supernatural?

HANNA

It had never occurred to me to use that word;——but now you mention it . . . he does make a highly——well, what shall I call it?——spiritual impression?——a very strange impression,——he does. As if he did not belong to this world.

KLARA

Ah! And you feel that, too?

HANNA

Yes, I certainly do!

KLARA

Do you know, that I may lie drawn up together, with my legs to my breast, and my arms . . . no, I dare not show you; or it would very likely come back . . . I may lie like that for whole days, when he is away, without being able to lay my limbs down again. You can imagine, it is terrible! Once ——he had gone over the fells; Oh, those journeys over the fells!——there I lay for eight

——whole——days, like that. And no sooner
did he stand there in the doorway, and I
looked at him and he looked at me, than my
arms and legs began to unbend, and he came
and passed his hand over them, and I lay as
straight as I am now ! And so it is repeatedly,
over and over again ! and if only he is in the
room, it passes from me.

HANNA

How extraordinary !

KLARA

What do you say to this, that the sick, that
is to say those that have real faith, and
were sick,——this has not happened once, but
hundreds of times,——when he came and
prayed with them, became quite well !

HANNA

Really well ?

KLARA

Perfectly well ! Yes, and what do you say
to this, that the sick, whom he has not been
able to visit,——for the distances here are so
great !——he has written to, that on such
and such a day and at such and such an hour,
he would pray for them and they must pray
then too ;——and from the same hour their sick-

ness has taken another turn! That is true! I
have many instances!

HANNA

Wonderful!——But you have never written
to me about this.

KLARA

I knew you Americans too well! Do you
think I would have exposed him to your
doubt?——

There is a pastor's widow here——Ah, you
must see her! She lives close by. She is the
most venerable old woman I can imagine!——
She had been lame for fifteen years when Sang
came here; and that is five-and-twenty years
ago. Now she goes to church every Sunday!
And she will soon be a hundred years old.

HANNA

He cured her?

KLARA

Simply by praying and making her pray!
You cannot imagine what *his* prayers are.
And then there is the case of Aagaat Florvaagen. That indeed is the most marvellous
of all. She lay dead before our eyes. He
takes one of her hands in his, and lays his
other hand on her heart and warms it, and
then she begins to breathe. She lives now

with the old widow——close by us!——I could lie here until to-morrow and go on telling and telling you about it. There is a glamour about him both in this place and far away, for thousands of believers all over the land, there has never been anything like it. And now it is beginning to spread abroad so much, that we are not left a day in peace.

HANNA

Then I also may be able to see this,——what you are talking of,——while I am with you?

KLARA

As sure as I lie here and can only raise myself on my elbows.

HANNA

Then why cannot his miraculous power help you, Klara? Why did he not heal you long ago?

KLARA

——There is a particular reason for that.——

HANNA

But you will tell me?

KLARA

No.——Yes, I mean. But afterwards. You must open a window again! It is so suffocating in here. More air, please!

HANNA

All right.   [*She opens one of the top windows.*]

KLARA

He ought to be here soon now. He *is* away a long time to-day. If I could only smell the scent of the flowers. A great many must have come into blossom after the rain. It is almost seven o'clock ; almost on the stroke of seven.

HANNA

[*Looks at her watch.*]   Yes, it is.

KLARA

Since I have been lying here, I always know what time it is.——I must feel one breath of fresh air.——Perhaps the wind has fallen ?——You do not answer me ?

HANNA

No, I did not hear what you said. I cannot recover from my amazement.

KLARA

Yes, it is indeed the most wonderful thing in our country,——perhaps in our time.

HANNA

What do the people say ? What do the peasants think of him ?

KLARA

I believe, it would have made twenty times
——a hundred times——more sensation at any
other place than just here. Here, it comes as
a matter of course !

HANNA

But, Klara ! a miracle is a miracle ?

KLARA

Yes, for us. But there is something in
nature here, which calls out the abnormal
in men also. Here nature itself is beyond
all ordinary bounds. We have night almost
the whole winter. We have day almost the
whole summer——and then the sun above the
horizon both night and day. You have seen
it at night? Do you know, that behind the
sea mists it appears three, and even four
times as large as at others? And its effects
of colour on the sky and the mountains and
the sea ! From the deepest glowing crimson
to the softest, most delicate, golden white.——
And the colours of the northern lights over
the sky in winter ! Although they are fainter
yet they take such wild forms, and suffer such
restless movement, such unceasing change !
And then the other wonders of nature !
Flocks of birds in millions; 'shoals of fish

that would reach from Paris to Strassburg,' as somebody wrote. You see these fells, that go straight up out of the sea? They are not like other mountains. And the whole Atlantic breaks upon them.

Naturally, the people's ideas are in harmony. They are boundless. Their legends, their stories are like piling up one land on another, and then rolling down icebergs from the North Pole upon them. Yes, you laugh. But listen to the legends here! Talk with the people, and you will soon understand how it is that pastor Adolf Sang is the man after their own heart! His faith suits the place! He came here with a large fortune and gave it almost all away. That was as it should be! That was Christianity! And now, when he travels for miles round to visit some poor sick man, and prays, they expand, as it were, and the light streams straight in upon them——! Sometimes they see him in impossible weather out on the sea, alone in a little, tiny boat; perhaps he has one or both of his children with him; for he has taken them with him ever since they were six years old! He works a miracle, perhaps, and then he is gone to another fishing-station——and there he works another! They seem to expect it of him. And more still! If I had not held

out against it, we should not have had now
enough to eat nor him alive,——nor perhaps
the children either. I will not even mention
myself, for I near the end.

HANNA

But then you have not held out ?——

KLARA

It may seem so. But I have. Not with
reproaches; that is of no good! No, I have
to invent something,——continually something new, every time; or else he finds it out.
Oh, it is hopeless!

HANNA

Invent something, do you say ?

KLARA

He is wanting in one whole sense, the
sense of Reality. He never sees anything
but what he wishes to see. Therefore, for
instance, nothing evil in any one. That is to
say, he sees it well enough, but he pays no
heed to it. 'I hold to the good in mankind,'
he says. And when he speaks to them, they
are all good, absolutely all! When he looks
at them with his child-like eyes,——who could
be otherwise? But it all goes wrong! He
ruins us on such people.

In this respect he is beyond all restraint,
you see, both in great things and small. If he
were allowed he would take the last thing we
had,——all we had to eat for the morrow,
——and say, 'God will return it to us; for
He has commanded us to do so.'

When such a storm is raging that the most
experienced seamen will not go out in a ship,
to say nothing of the pastor's long-boat,——
then he will start off in a little four-oar,——
perhaps with the little child in the stern!

Once he crossed over the fell in a mist and
wandered there for three days and three
nights without tasting food or drink. They
went out to search for him, and brought him
back to human habitations. And then he
wanted the week after to make the same
journey, in a mist, again! There was a sick
man who expected him!

HANNA

But can he endure it all?

KLARA

He can endure anything. He falls asleep
like a tired child, and sleeps, and sleeps, and
sleeps. Then he wakes up, eats, and starts
afresh. He is perfectly unique; for he is perfectly innocent.

HANNA

How you do love him !

KLARA

Yes, it is the only thing that is left of me. All this trouble about the children has worn me out.

HANNA

About the children ?

KLARA

It was doing them harm, being here. Nothing was fixed and regular; they were getting unsettled. Never any obstacles to anything which was considered to be right! Never any intention, nothing but inspiration! They were grown up and could do little more than read and write.

And how I struggled to get them away! and since, for five years, to be able to keep them there and get them instruction! Ah! that has exhausted all my strength. Now it is ended.

HANNA

My poor Klara !

KLARA

You do not think . . . ? You are not *pitying* me ? *Me,* who have made the journey with the best man in all the world? with the purest heart of all mankind?

One lives shorter in this way——true. One cannot combine everything.

But change?——Hanna!

HANNA

Has he broken down all the rest of you?

KLARA

He has! just so! At least——he has not broken down every one; he was not allowed to do that. He would have broken himself down too if he had been allowed to do so. He has got beyond himself.

HANNA

Beyond himself? When he actually works miracles, and is continually delivered out of danger?

KLARA

Do you not think that the miracles come from the very fact of his being beyond himself?

HANNA

You frighten me! What do you mean?

KLARA

I mean, that the prophets were so too, both the Hebrew and the Heathen. They could do more than we in a certain direction, because they lacked so much in all other directions. Yes, I have often thought that.

HANNA

But do you not *believe*, then ?

KLARA

Believe ? Yes, what do you mean by that ? We sisters come of an old, nervous, sceptical family,——I may say, of an intellectual family. I admired Sang. He was unlike all other men, better than all others. I admired him, until I loved him. It was not his faith ; that was something entirely his own. How far I now believe as he does,——I do not know.

HANNA

You do not know ?

KLARA

I have been so harassed, you see, that I have never had time to make up my mind. Such things need time. And I have had enough to do to provide for us between the shock of one wave and the next. I was worn out with it only too soon. I was no longer fit to consider great questions.

I can scarcely distinguish right from wrong. I can roughly, of course,——but I mean, on more delicate points. I must go on as I can. And similarly with faith. I can do no more.

HANNA

He knows this?

KLARA

He knows everything. Do you think I hide anything from him?

HANNA

But does he not try to make you believe what he believes himself?

KLARA

Not in the least. The necessity of faith, to escape condemnation, he says, is God's business. Ours is sincerity. Then, we shall have faith enough——here or hereafter. Ah, he is a perfect man, throughout.

HANNA

But yet he labours to spread the faith?

KLARA

In his own way. Never, no, never with contention. He shows exactly the same consideration for all. Do you hear?——for all! Ah, there is no man like him!

HANNA

You look upon him now as you did in the first days of enchantment, even when your eyes have grown old.

KLARA

Yes, even when my eyes have grown old.

HANNA

But about your faith in his miracles . . . As a matter of fact you have no faith in them at all?

KLARA

What are you saying? There is nothing that exists in which I have such absolute faith!

HANNA

If you dare not let him go out of your sight in a tempest, and if you dare not trust that you will receive again what he would give away, even though it is your last, . . . then you have no faith in them.

KLARA

Before I would consent to any of those things, I would . . . Yes, and it is *there* that my strength lies, let me tell you.

HANNA

Ah! but that is not the strength of faith.

KLARA

No, no. But, if this is inconsistency—— what does it matter! We all have our inconsistencies——except him. For the rest, I will tell you, that to cast one's-self or one's children into the sea is more than faith; it is tempting God.

HANNA

Well, it seems to me that a miracle must take place just the same, whether our own life is at stake or that of other people.

KLARA

But to *put* one's-self in danger of one's life ?

HANNA

When it is done to save others ? ' That cannot be called tempting God.

KLARA

Look here,——talk no more of that ! I cannot do it. I only know, that if he wants to take the children's bread, and give it to bad, wicked men, or if he wants to go himself up into the mountains in a mist, or put out to sea in a tempest,——well, then I throw myself right in the way ! I do everything, absolutely everything I can conceive, to stop it !

Supposing he wished to do so now, . . . ? I have not been able to raise myself on my legs for many months; . . . but I could then ! I

could then! I am certain! Then, I too could
work a miracle. For I love him and his
children.

[*A long silence.*

HANNA

Is there nothing I can do for you?

KLARA

Let me have some *eau de Cologne*! Here
——over my temples. And let me smell it!
Some of what you gave me yesterday. A
little, quick! Cannot you draw the cork?—
There is the corkscrew! There, there!
And the lower window open!——The lower
one too!

HANNA

Yes, yes!

KLARA

Thank you! If the ground were not so
damp after the dreadful rain, I should like
to go out. Cannot you get the cork out?

HANNA

Yes, it is just coming.

KLARA

Screw it further in. Not too far. That is
right! That is right! Come!——No;——
jasmin!

HANNA

Jasmin?——no, nothing of the kind!

KLARA

Jasmin, jasmin!——It is he! I can hear
him! It is he! Thank God! I shall soon
be at peace——at peace. Oh! this is indeed
a blessing! It . . . is . . . he.

[*Sang comes in.*

The Second Scene

SANG

Good morning again!—— Good morning,
dear Hanna! To think that you are here!
——really here——
You do not have such mornings in America,
so full of scent and song. Nor anywhere else
in the world!

KLARA

But my flowers?

SANG

Do you know what has happened to me to-
day, Klara?

KLARA

You have given them away?

SANG

No. [*Laughing.*] No, not this time, as Torden-
skjold said. That is wicked of you! Here
have we been grumbling and growling at this
' incessant,' ' terrible ' rain, dreading landslips
and slides from the fell——and all sorts of
disasters. . . . And yet the rain has only
worked a marvel of loving-kindness! When I
saw the sun to-day at last and went out . . .
ah! what a world of flowers I entered! I
never saw anything like them before this
year! I went out into a wealth of perfume
and colour. . . . All at once I fell into such
a mood, that it really seemed a shame to go
and trample down the grass, that stood there
and caused one such great gladness. And so
I turned aside and found a field-path and
walked along it and looked down into the
flowers' wet eyes. There was such a crowding
among them, you cannot think! Such an
instinct of self-preservation in the crowd!
Such aspiration! The least among them
strove to stretch out its neck to the sun with
the rest. So wide open and greedy! Really
some of them were in blossom so early, that I
believe the rascals will be sending off their
pollen to woo before the day is over! I saw
some humble bees already! They did not
know where to fly amid all the currents of

scent! For one thousand only smelt sweeter and invited them more eagerly than the next thousand, and there were thousands of thousands! Yes, now things will go well. Is there not individuality in this million-fold life? There is indeed! And so I could not take any of them.

But I have something else for you to-day!

KLARA

[*Who has been making signs to her sister, while he has been talking.*]
Have you?

SANG

I too am going to try to open my calix to-day.

KLARA

What do you mean, dear?

SANG

Ah, you did not think so ill of me, as that I can conceal anything; but I can!

KLARA

I have noticed for a long time that there was something——?

SANG

No, have you really? For I really have been silent, this time.

But if I have not been so alarmed about your illness as all the rest, there has been a special reason for it.

KLARA

What is it?

HANNA

Yes, what is it? She is getting so excited.

SANG

I will make haste!——I have helped so many and cannot help her, because I cannot really pray with her, dear heretic! And I have no power in the matter, if the sick do not pray with me,——at least, when they can pray. So I wrote to our children to come. And yesterday evening, when I took them up to bed so early, I told them why,—— it was, that they might sleep their sleep out to the end and then help me to-day at seven o'clock and pray by their mother's bed!

KLARA

My dear, my dear!

SANG

We will lay a chain of prayer round you! One of our children at your feet, and one at your head, and I straight in front! Then we shall not cease, until you fall asleep! Not before! No, not before! And then we shall repeat our prayer, until you rise up and go about amongst us. That is what we shall do.

KLARA

Dear Adolf!

HANNA

What did the children say?

SANG

Ah, you should have seen them! They were so deeply moved. I assure you, they grew as white as that sheet. And then they looked at one another.

Then I understood, they must be alone.

I see it moves you too. You close your eyes. Perhaps you too wish to be alone now? ——Yes, we are about to receive a visit. A great visit! It is right that we should make ourselves ready!——What o'clock is it?

HANNA

It is past seven.

SANG

No, it cannot be; or else they would be here.——You have forgotten to set your watch by our time.

HANNA

No, I have not.

SANG

Then you have not set it right, my dear Hanna. Do you think that grown-up children, who are going to pray by their mother's bed, oversleep themselves?

HANNA

I will go up to them.

SANG

No, no, no! They must have these last moments alone! I understand it.

HANNA

They shall not hear me. I will only just look in. *[She goes.*

SANG

Well, be very quiet!

THE THIRD SCENE

SANG

It *is* pleasant, that she is so much interested.

KLARA

Dear!

SANG

There is something troubled in your voice?

Now be hopeful! I tell you, I have never felt more sure. And you know Who it is that gives that feeling.

Klara!——My beloved Klara!

[*He kneels by her bed.*

Before we meet in this great prayer, you must suffer me to thank you! I have thanked God for you to-day. In all this glory of the spring-time have I given thanks. There was such infinite joy about me and within me. I went over in outline all that we have lived through together. Do you know, I believe I love you all the more, because you do not share my faith entirely;——for that very reason you are still more unceasingly in my thoughts. Your devotion to me is the devotion of all your whole being, your will, —— it flows from nothing else. And that you stand by me and still hold your own truth, I am proud of *that*.

But now, when I think, that——without believing as I do——you have given your life for me,——

KLARA

Adolf!

SANG

I will put my hand over your mouth, if you talk. It is my turn now!——Ah, this is a great thing that you have done. We——we gave our faith ; but you have given your life. What perfect trust you must have in me! How I love you !

Whenever the zeal of my faith frightened you, and you trembled for me or for our children's future, and then perhaps did not weigh what you did, . . . I knew you had not strength left to do it better.

KLARA

No, I had not !

SANG

The fault is mine. I have not understood how to spare you.

KLARA

Adolf !

SANG

I know it is so. You have sacrificed yourself inch by inch. Not from faith, not from hope of reward here or hereafter ;——from love alone. How I love you !

I wanted to tell you this to-day. If Hanna had not gone out, I should have asked her to leave me alone with you for a little while.

I thank you ! to-day is your great day. In a few moments our children will be here.

Ah ! let me kiss you as I kissed you on the first day of all !

The Fourth Scene

SANG

Well?

HANNA

It is past seven o'clock.

KLARA

I knew it.

SANG

Is it past seven?——But the children?

HANNA

They were asleep.

SANG

They were asleep?

KLARA

I knew it.

HANNA

Elias was drest. He had thrown himself on his bed, as if he had only wanted to rest and not to sleep, but nevertheless he had fallen asleep. Rakel was asleep with her hands folded over the counterpane. She heard nothing.

SANG

I have asked too much of the children.—— I can never cease from doing so.

HANNA

Yes, they had scarcely slept for two days
and nights; in fact, not since we met.

SANG

But what did God purpose in giving me
such power just to-day? And in making me
so certain?——I must try and learn that. [*He
goes.*] Let me leave you for a moment, dear!——
and dear Hanna!——Why just to-day——?

THE FIFTH SCENE

KLARA

Did you wake them?

HANNA

Of course I did.——Do you know what I
believe is the matter?

KLARA

O God, yes!——Oh! I am beginning to
tremble so.

HANNA

Is there anything to be done for it?

KLARA

No; unless I can manage to conquer it

myself.——Ah !——There was something in their eyes yesterday.   I understand it now.

HANNA

They no longer hold their father's faith.

KLARA

They no longer hold their father's faith. ——How they must have struggled and suffered, poor, dear children ! They love and honour him more than anything else in the world !

HANNA

That was why they were so quiet yesterday.

KLARA

Yes, that was why they were so much moved by the least thing !——Ah, and that is why Rakel wrote to ask you to come.   Some ought to be here,——and she dared not come herself.

HANNA

No doubt you are right.——How they must have struggled against it !

KLARA

Ah, poor, poor children !

HANNA

Here is Elias !

KLARA

Is he here?

ELIAS

[*Throws himself on his knees by his mother's bed with his face between his hands.*
O mother!

KLARA

Yes, yes!——I know it.

ELIAS

You know it? It could not be worse!

KLARA

No, it could not be worse.

ELIAS

When he said yesterday evening, that at seven o'clock to-day . . .

KLARA

. . . Hush, hush! I cannot bear it.

HANNA

Your mother cannot bear it.

ELIAS

No, no!——I knew, it must come. In one way or another. I knew, it must come at last.

HANNA

Can you bear to hear it?

KLARA

I must hear it.——Tell me—— !

HANNA

What is it?

KLARA

Elias . . . are not you there?

ELIAS

I am here, mother.

KLARA

Rakel?

ELIAS

What do you mean, mother?

KLARA

Where is Rakel?

ELIAS

She is getting up now. She stayed awake with me until twelve o'clock last night; and then she could do no more.

KLARA

Child, how,——oh, how——did this come
about—— ?

ELIAS

That we lost our father's faith ?

KLARA

. . . that you lost your father's faith, child ?

THE SEVENTH SCENE

SANG

Have you lost your faith ?——My son ?——
Have *you* lost your faith ?

HANNA

Look at Klara !——Klara !

SANG

[*Hastens to her. He lays his hands upon her.*
It is ceasing. It will not come——By God's
grace !

KLARA

It is passing away——Only, hold me, dear !

SANG

I will hold you.

KLARA

And do not let me cry ! Oh !——

SANG

No, no, you must not cry ! [*He leans right over her and kisses her.*] Be strong !——Klara ! ——There, there ! You must not be distressed. You must remember how distressed they have been. They have tried to spare us in all their pain and conflict, and shall we not spare them ?

KLARA

Yes.

SANG

That was why you were seized with that convulsion. We must think what we are doing. Or else perhaps we might have shown bitterness towards them. Especially I in my zeal. Where is Rakel ?

HANNA

She is coming directly. She stayed awake with Elias until twelve o'clock last night.

SANG

Children ! Children !——How could you ——? —— No, no ! I will not know about it.

You were always true. If you have done it,——you *must*.

ELIAS

I *must.* But it has been terrible.

SANG

You found your faith too easily here with me. I am only a man of feeling. Perhaps *this* is your entrance upon a faith that can never be lost.

ELIAS

I feel like a criminal ;——but I am not !

SANG

Do you think that I doubt for a moment, my son ? You must not make that mistake, because I cannot quite control myself. That comes from my having built so much upon your faith.—Then it must take time before I . . . No, no, no ! Forgive me, Elias ! Indeed, you could not help it.

[*Rakel comes in, but retreats shyly a few steps into the background. He sees her.*

Rakel !——O Rakel ! [*She comes and falls on her knees.*] Ever since you were quite little, you have taught me more faith than any book.——

How can this be possible? No, if they have won her over,——still I must know how !—— For that any one could take *you* from me . . .

RAKEL

Not from *you*, father!

SANG

Forgive me! Ah! I did not mean to wound you.——Come hither to me!

[*She throws herself in his arms.*

I promise you, my children, that from henceforth I will never mention it again.——But first I must know——you cannot wonder at that?——how this came about.

ELIAS

If you were to talk with me about it for whole days, father,——I should not have finished it.

SANG

Nay, I am not fit for that. I cannot reason about faith. I do not comprehend it at all.

ELIAS

But still, you will hear me?

SANG

If it can be any comfort to you,——that is another thing. Then you know I will.

But can you not tell me shortly?——Quite shortly.

What was it that made you . . . that——
well——that decided you, child?

ELIAS

I can tell you very shortly. Rakel and I
did not find that Christians were such ás you
had taught us.

SANG

But child——?

ELIAS

You had sent us to the best that you knew.
And they were the best. But Rakel and
I were soon agreed, and it was she who first
said so :—'There is only one Christian, and
that is father.'

SANG

My child!

ELIAS

If the others had·been a little more or a
little less of what you are, a part of it,——
then we should not have felt so disappointed.
But they are something quite different;——
totally distinct.

SANG

What do you mean?

ELIAS

Their Christianity is mere conformity.
Both in life and doctrine they bow before

circumstances,——those existing at their place and time,——institutions, customs, prejudices, economic conditions and so forth.

They have found out loopholes in doctrine so that it can be adapted to the times.

SANG

Is not that severe?

ELIAS

You seek for its most ideal element and follow after that. That is what makes the difference.

SANG

But what has this difference to do with you, dear child?

ELIAS

It set us thinking, father.——Can you wonder at it?

SANG

Think as much as you will, if only you do not judge.

RAKEL

I do not think we did that. And do you know why? Because we saw that their doctrine was as natural to them as your doctrine is to you.

SANG

Well——?

ELIAS

But what then is Christianity? It is certainly not theirs?

SANG

Suppose it is not? What harm is there in it? If they practise it as they understand it?

RAKEL

Then is Christianity something which only one in a million can reach, dear father?

ELIAS

Are all the rest to be mere dabblers in it?

SANG

What do you call a Christian?

ELIAS

I call him only a Christian who has learnt from Jesus the mystery of Perfection, and strives after it in all things.

SANG

Ah! that seems to me a lovely definition! You have some of your mother's delicate perception.——Ah, it has always been my great dream, that one day you . .

No, no, no!——I promised you, children . . .
And I will keep to it. You said—— That
is true; that is very, very good!

But, my son, cannot every one be allowed to
try to become a Christian without being called
a dabbler on that account? What? Is it not
thus that faith suffices for our insufficiency?
This merit of one for the frailty of thousands?

ELIAS

There you name it! When we strive with
all our hearts,——then it is that faith suffices.

SANG

Well then——?

ELIAS

Only one man carries this into practice,——
and that is you. The rest . . . No, do not
be afraid! I do not say it in order to find
fault. What right have I to do that? The
rest——either deduct so much from it that
they can take it quietly,——it suits them to do
so;——or really try——and strain themselves!
Yes, that is the word.

RAKEL

Yes, that is the word.
And then it was, father, that I said to
Elias: 'But if these ideals suit the conditions
and powers of mankind so little, even in these

days, they certainly cannot come from an omniscient Being.

SANG

Was it *you*, who said that?——

ELIAS

We could no longer get rid of Rakel's doubts. And so we gave ourselves up to study. We followed back these ideals in history——beyond our own era.

RAKEL

They are all——all of them——much older than Christianity, father?

SANG

I know it, my child.

ELIAS

They were taught long before, by Mystics . . .

SANG

. . . by Eastern and by Greek Mystics in an age of doubt——an age in which the best only yearned for a land——far, far off——where all things are made new. I know that, my children.

So it was here you fell? Good God!

As if the land of renewing, the kingdom of the millennium were not quite as true, because it is an ancient, incalculably ancient, eastern dream,

If it has kept men waiting so long for it that feeble souls begin to call it an impossible dream——and the cravings that lead thither, impossible ideals, . . . what does that show?

Nothing about what is taught, but much about those who teach it. Yes, alas!——much about those who teach it.

I will not talk of them, I will only say, what happened to myself. I saw Christianity crawling——very cautiously——avoiding all the greater heights. Why does it do so? I asked myself. Is it because, if it rose up to its full height, it would lift things off their hinges?

Is it Christianity which is impossible, or mankind which is faint-hearted? If only one were bold,——would there not then be thousands bold? And so I felt that I ought to try and be that one. And that, I think, every one must try. Yes; otherwise, he has no faith. For faith is to know, that to faith nothing is impossible,——and then to show the faith!

Do I say this to boast? Indeed, I say it in order to blame myself. For although I have now built so high and received such great grace, I too still fall, again and again, from God.

Have I not been going about now again

thinking it impossible to save her who lies there, alone ? Have I not doubted, and waited for others' help ?

Therefore has God taken their help from me. Therefore did He permit that you also should fall at 'the Impossible' and come and tell me so. For thus should His hour be prepared. Now He will show to all of us, what *is* possible !

Ah,——I came here and did not understand! Now I understand. I shall do it, alone ! Now I have received the command ; now I *can*.

For this reason the great grace of preparedness came just to-day. All things work together.

Klara, do you hear ? It is no longer I that speak ; it is the great certainty within me, ——and you know from Whom that always comes ! *[He kneels by her.*

Klara, my beautiful wife, why should not you be as dear to God as any of those who believe completely ? As if God were not the Father of all ! God's Love to man is not a privilege of believers. The privilege of believers is to feel His Love and to rejoice in it——to make the impossible possible in His name.

You patient, stedfast woman ! I go from you now to prove it. *[He stands up.*

Yes ! To prove it ! I go into the church,

children; for I must be alone. I shall not
come out again, until I have got from God's
hands sleep for your mother, and after sleep,
health; so that she may rise up and go about
amongst us.

Do not be afraid! I feel He will! He
will not give it me at once; for this time I
have doubted. But I shall wait patiently for
the mighty, merciful God.——Farewell!

> [*He throws himself down over her for a
> short time and prays.*

Farewell!

> [*He kisses her. She lies motionless. He
> stands up.*

Thank you, my children! Now you have
helped me indeed. More than heart could
know.

Now I will myself ring in my prayer. So
you will know at the first stroke of the bell
that I have begun to pray for mother. Peace
be with you!

HANNA

> [*Has involuntarily opened the door for him.
> Sang goes out.*

This . . . This is . . . [*She bursts into tears.*

ELIAS

I must see . . I must see him go in.

> [*He goes out.*

RAKEL

[*Forward.*]　　Mother !——Mother !

HANNA

Do not speak to her ! She looks at you ;
but do not speak to her !

RAKEL

I am afraid.

HANNA

Where I stand, I can see your father. He
is almost at the church now.——Come !

RAKEL

No ! . . . No, I cannot bear it. I am so
afraid.——Mother ! She looks at me ; but
she does not answer.——Mother !

HANNA

Hush, Rakel !　　　　[*The bell begins to ring.*

RAKEL

[*Falls on her knees. A little later she ex-
　claims in a hushed voice :*
God !——Hanna !

HANNA

What is it ?

RAKEL

Mother is asleep !

HANNA

Asleep?

RAKEL

Mother is asleep!

HANNA

Really and truly?

RAKEL

I must find Elias. I must tell Elias.

[*She goes out.*

HANNA

She sleeps like a child. O God!

[*She kneels down.*
[*A continuous roar is heard, growing louder
and louder every instant; gathering fearful
power. Outside, shrieks. The house
trembles. The roar grows louder still.*

RAKEL

[*Outside.*] The mountains are falling! [*She
shrieks; then she comes rushing in.*] The mountains are falling over the church! Over us!
Right over the church! Over us! Over
father, and us! They are rolling, rushing,
——it is growing dark,——Oh!

[*She cowers down and turns away her face.*

ELIAS

[*Outside.*]   Father !——Father !——Oh !

HANNA

[*Over her sister's bed.*]   It is coming !——It is coming !

> [*The roar is at its height.   Then, little by little, it diminishes.   Then the church bell is heard again above it.*

HANNA

[*Jumping up.*]   It is still ringing !   He is safe !

RAKEL

He is safe !

ELIAS

[*Outside.*]   Father is alive !   [*Nearer.*]   The church is standing.   [*In the room.*]   The church is standing.   Father is alive.   Just by the church the slide swerved,—turned to the left.   He is alive, he is ringing, O God !

> [*He throws himself down over his mother's bed.*

RAKEL

[*Comes in.*]   Elias !   Mother——?

HANNA

She is asleep !

ELIAS

[*Springs up.*]   Is she asleep?

RAKEL

Yes, she is asleep.——
[*The church bell still sounds*

HANNA

She still sleeps, peacefully.

THE SECOND ACT

*A little timber room. In the back wall is a door, lead-
ing on to a veranda. The door is wide open;
through it is visible a narrow landscape shut in
by a bare mountain. In the right-hand wall is a
door. In the left a large window. Over the door
leading on to the veranda is a gilt crucifix let into
a cross, over which is a sheet of glass. In front
to the left is a sofa with a table before it, on the
table are some books. Chairs stand against the
walls.*

THE FIRST SCENE

*[Elias comes in hurriedly from the veranda; he is
very restless. He has on linen trousers and thin
shoes. Above, nothing but a shirt; no hat.
He stops, goes to the window and listens. A
psalm, sung by a man's voice at a little dis-
tance can be distinctly heard. Elias is deeply
agitated.*

*Rakel comes in softly at the door to the right, which
was shut. She shuts it again after her. Her
brother makes a sign to her to stop and listen.]*

RAKEL

[Who is also agitated, says softly :] Let me
open the door that leads in to mother.

ELIAS

[*Softly.*]   Has mother awaked, then ?

RAKEL

No ; but I am sure that she can hear father.
[*She disappears to the right ; comes quietly
in again and leaves the door open behind
her ; she says softly :*

She smiled.

ELIAS

[*Softly.*]   O Rakel !

RAKEL

[*Agitated.*]   Elias !——Do not say anything ;
——I cannot bear it.

ELIAS

Look out there, Rakel !——Could there be
anything more beautiful ? Hundreds of people
kneeling in the deepest silence round the
church ; and he praying and singing within,
perfectly unconscious that there is any one
outside. The windows are open, but they are
too high for him to see out of them. And the
people striving with all their might to make
no sound lest they should disturb him !

Look ! He talked about a chain of prayer.
All those people round the church,——that is
a chain of prayer.

RAKEL

Yes. [*They listen to the singing. It ceases.*]
He is singing often to-day.

ELIAS

Shut the doors now! I have so much to
tell you. I have been here twice to look for
you.

RAKEL

[*Goes out softly to the right; comes in again and
shuts the door after her. She says louder :*
Still more people have come during the
afternoon.

ELIAS

And they are still coming continually,——
from miles round! You cannot see them all;
a large part of them are further away, among
the trees, listening to the lay preachers. They
do not disturb father there. And the people
go to and fro, between the trees and the
church.——But do you see, down on the
beach—— ?

RAKEL

No, what is it? The fields are getting
black with people! What is it?

ELIAS

It is the mission-ship that has arrived.

RAKEL

The mission-ship?

ELIAS

Do you not know, that all the Eastlanders have hired a steamer for the great mission conference in town? It lies here now in the fjord.

RAKEL

Here?

ELIAS

Here!

RAKEL

But what has it come here for?

ELIAS

For the miracle! When our delegates——Pastor Kröjer and the other——went on board at the calling station out at sea——

RAKEL

——Well——?

ELIAS

——and told what had happened here yesterday, and that father was still in the church alone praying,——

RAKEL

——I understand now!

ELIAS

——Not a single man would go any further !
they insisted on coming here ! The Bishop
and the Clergy urged them to keep their
word and go on to their appointment ; but
they would come here ! So the rest were
obliged to yield. And now they are here.

RAKEL

And the Clergy too ?

ELIAS

The Bishop and the Clergy——of course !

RAKEL

They are not coming in here are they ?——
Elias, you ought to be rather differently dressed.

ELIAS

I cannot bear my clothes on.

RAKEL

You cannot bear them——?

ELIAS

They burn me. And then I have a longing
. . . well, as it were, to pass through the air.
I cannot describe it to you ; but sometimes I
seem as if I must be able to do it.

RAKEL

But, Elias——!

ELIAS

There he is ! There he goes !

RAKEL

Who ? That man, there ?

ELIAS

It *is* the man ?——Yes, it is ! They carried him here this morning, mortally sick; and now he walks; there ! you can see him.

It was to-day, when father first began to sing. No one had expected he would sing; we all burst into tears together. Then the sick man rose up of himself. We did not observe it until he was going about among us.——

Mother will rise up too, Rakel ! I can observe it before my eyes !

RAKEL

She will rise up. I expect it every moment; but I shudder at the thought.

You stare at me, Elias ?

ELIAS

Yes,——for sometimes, when you speak, your words seem to me to run in verse. And also when others speak.

RAKEL

But, Elias—— ?

ELIAS

Sometimes again——as now, for instance
——I only hear the sound; and no meaning.
For I hear in the same breath something,——
something that is not spoken.

RAKEL

That is not spoken?

ELIAS

Oftenest, father calling ;——calling me by
name,——as he did yesterday morning. [*Ex-
citedly.*] He had some meaning when he
gave me my name. It sounds and upbraids
——yes, in his voice.

Sometimes I am driven hither and thither
incessantly! And in the midst of it I feel
impelled to rush into the greatest danger.
I am certain I should come out of it un-
hurt. No, do not be afraid! There is none
here.

RAKEL

Elias, come and sit with me in mother's
room! There is peace there, with mother.

ELIAS

I cannot.——Rakel! answer me before God,
——try your last, subtlest doubt, and answer
me: is this a miracle that we have lived to
see here?

RAKEL

Good God, Elias,——why always that?

ELIAS

But is it not terrible, that the only two, who still perhaps doubt, are his own children? I would give my life to be certain of it now.

RAKEL

Elias, say no more! I entreat you!

ELIAS

Only tell me what you believe! The land-slip——? That is too great to be a mere coincidence. Is not that true? And mother's sleep? Directly he began to ring,——sleep! And sleep, in spite of the landslip! Sleep, as long as he prays!

Is not this a miracle? Why then is not the other also a miracle, a great miracle?

RAKEL

I almost believe it is, Elias.

ELIAS

You do?

RAKEL

But I am quite as much afraid of it, for all that.

ELIAS

Afraid of it, if it is a miracle? But then you cannot believe that it *is* a miracle?

RAKEL

Yes, I can.

ELIAS

For certainly *that* cannot be merely his magnetic power of healing? Or the strength of his personality? No, it is more than that! Is it a miracle? Do you feel certain?

RAKEL

I cannot think of that now. It is in order to have peace from it, that I take refuge with mother. Mother's truthfulness seems to fill the whole room and deaden such questions.

There is something else to be thought of now, Elias.

ELIAS

Something else?

RAKEL

After this! What will come after this,—— when she has risen up? For that is not the end of it. In the end——

ELIAS

In the end—— ?

RAKEL

In the end it will be a question of their lives !   [*She bursts into tears.*

ELIAS

Rakel——?   O God !

RAKEL

Mother has no more strength to withstand anything.   And he will go on——especially now !

ELIAS

What with ?

RAKEL

With this,——whatever it is !

ELIAS

But supposing it is a miracle, Rakel?   Why should you be frightened, then ?

RAKEL

I cannot foresee the consequences to father and mother,——and to us all.   Ah ! you do not understand me at all ?

ELIAS

No.

RAKEL

No !   It is all the same to me, whatever it is; it unhinges us.   It will undo us in the end.

ELIAS

The miracle ?

RAKEL

Yes, yes.   It is no blessing ; it is a terror !
——Elias !

[*She pulls him further back into the room.*

ELIAS

What is it ?

RAKEL

There is a man standing close under the
window staring in.——A strange man, very
pale.

ELIAS

——in a coat buttoned to the chin —— ?

RAKEL

Yes.——[*With a suppressed scream.*]   Why
there he is actually standing in the room !

[*She goes out backwards as if she were re-
treating before a spectre, and takes refuge
with her mother.*

ELIAS

In the room ?——Here ?

[*At the same moment a stranger comes into
the veranda from the left, he crosses the
threshold, stands still, and looks about him.*

The Second Scene

ELIAS

[*As the stranger makes his appearance.*]　There
he is!

THE STRANGER

Excuse me——?

ELIAS

Who are you?

THE STRANGER

Need that make any difference?——

ELIAS

I have seen you about since yesterday.

THE STRANGER

Yes.　I came here over the mountain.

ELIAS

Over the mountain?

THE STRANGER

I stood above and saw the slide fall.

ELIAS

Really!

THE STRANGER

And heard the bell ring. And to-day I have seen the sick man, who rose up when your father sang.——And now I ask : is it there, within, where your mother sleeps?

ELIAS

Yes. Not in the first room ; in the next.

THE STRANGER

But if she rises up, . . . then she will come in here——? She will go towards the church, where he is——? Is not that so ? Then she will come ? Here ?

ELIAS

Well, now you mention it——

THE STRANGER

And so I ask you,——I entreat you—— : might I be here ?——Wait here ? See it ? I have had such a burning desire. I can resist no longer.

I will not come in before I feel driven to do so. I will not sit here and take up room,—— and be in the way. But if I feel irresistibly driven to come in and wait here and see . . . have I your leave to come ?

ELIAS

Yes.

THE STRANGER

Thank you !

I must tell you : this day decides my life.

[*He goes out by the veranda to the right.*

THE THIRD SCENE

ELIAS

This day shall decide my life ! [*Kröjer comes in by the veranda from the left.*] Kröjer, did you see that man ? The man there, on the right ?

KRÖJER

Yes. Who was he ?

ELIAS

You do not know him ?

KRÖJER

No.

ELIAS

At any rate he is a wonderful man.——This day shall decide my life ! My God ! That is the word for me !

KRÖJER

I expected, Elias, that this day would be a great day for you.

Indeed, who can withstand what is going forward here?

Only those hundreds of people in prayer round the church, and he within, not knowing it! I cannot conceive anything more beautiful.

ELIAS

Is it not?——Oh, I will cast away all my doubts and fears;——this day shall decide! What a saying that was.

I have fought and suffered without reaching further. And now it is freely given to me! I shall soon have more peace.——Let us talk together!

KRÖJER

No,——not now. I have an errand to you.

ELIAS

To me?——Who from?

KRÖJER

I have come back here with the mission ship.

ELIAS

I know it.

KRÖJER

And now the Bishop and Clergy ask whether they can borrow this room for an hour?

ELIAS

What for?

KRÖJER

They are anxious to discuss, how they are to act with regard to what is happening here. And we do not know any other place where we can be alone.——Yes, do not be so surprised. We professionals, we of the preaching trade, must endeavour to consider such things more critically than others, you know.

ELIAS

But there will be a long, tedious wrangle here?

KRÖJER

Which may end in harmony! Who can resist miraculous power?

ELIAS

You are right! But in here, you know? As it were, thrust in between father and mother?——And supposing father begins to sing again? In that case we shall not be able to open the door in to mother?

KRÖJER

What answer do you think your mother or your father would have given them?

ELIAS

Yes, unconditionally! You are right!

They shall have the room.——But spare me this——?

KRÖJER

I will arrange it. Both the doors in to your mother are shut?

ELIAS

Yes.

KRÖJER

Then I will shut this window and the door too, when the rest have come in.

ELIAS

Let them shut themselves in! I will go out and find sympathy from the people yonder. They wait with confidence for something great to happen to-day;——and surely they will not wait long in vain. [*He goes out.*

KRÖJER

[*Follows him.*] Shall we pray for it, Elias?

ELIAS

Yes. I will try, now!
[*They both go out to the left.*

The Fourth Scene

KRÖJER

[*Coming in again from the left.*] Allow me!
[*He comes first and shuts the window. Mean-
while the Bishop and Clergy come in.
Kröjer goes back and shuts the door.*

BLANK

Since you are an intimate of this house,
could not you procure us some refreshment?

THE BISHOP

We make rather a ludicrous figure,——I
know. But the fact is, we were dreadfully
sea-sick.

BREJ

We could not keep anything upon our
stomachs.

THE BISHOP

At last, when we got into smooth water,
and they were just going to cook us something to eat . . .

BREJ

. . . came the miracle!

FALK

I am so fearfully hungry.

KRÖJER

I am afraid that no one here, either, has
had any thought for food to-day ;——but I
will go and see.   [*He goes out.*

JENSEN

I have regular hallucinations about eating.
I have read of such things; but one reads of
so much one does not believe.
It is ptarmigan especially that I see.

FALK

Ptarmigan!

JENSEN

I smell it too ; roast ptarmigan !

BLANK

Ptarmigan ?——Indeed ! ?

SEVERAL

Will they give us ptarmigan ?

KRÖJER

[*Comes in again and says while still in the
doorway :*
I am sorry to say I have been into both the
kitchen and the larder, but they are empty.
And there is no one about.

BREJ

Not a single soul ?

FALK

I am so frightfully hungry.

THE BISHOP

Do not let us make too ludicrous a figure either, my friends. We must submit to the inevitable. Let us set to work.

Be so kind as to be seated !

[*He himself sits down on the sofa ; the rest take chairs.*

We must endeavour, as briefly and quietly as possible——for we know that this house is the dwelling of a sick person——to come to an understanding as to how we are to act in this matter.

I have always been of the opinion, that in the face of any such movement the clergy should —— as a rule —— hold themselves neutral ; neither co-operating nor opposing, until the movement has spread so widely that some judgment can be formed upon it.

To-day, therefore, I was heartily desirous that we should continue our journey. But we did not continue our journey.

THE CLERGY

[*Muttering among themselves.*] We did not continue our journey. No, we did not continue our journey.

THE BISHOP

They all insisted on coming hither, where,

so to speak, the miraculous power was believed to reside. ˜And I do not blame them for it.

But if we are in their company, on the same ship, they will want our opinion. When we arrive at the Conference, they will also want our opinion there.——Well, what is our opinion?

KRÖJER

Permit me, with all respect : either we believe in a miraculous power and shall act accordingly ; or we do not believe in it and shall act according to that.

THE BISHOP

Hm ?——There is a third course, my young friend.

THE CLERGY

[*Muttering among themselves.*] There is a third course ! Certainly, certainly, there is a third course !

THE BISHOP

The older and more experienced a man becomes, the more difficulty he has in forming a conviction,——especially on supernatural matters.——In the present case, time and circumstance scarcely even allow of an investigation. And suppose we arrive at various conclusions ? In these times of scepticism, what would be the effect of a division among the clergy on the question of the miraculous power; and whether miracles are being performed at the present time at certain places in the Norlands, or not?

I see that our venerable brother Blank desires to speak.

BLANK

If I have rightly apprehended your Reverence's meaning, we are not called upon in the first instance to decide whether a miracle is wrought here or not. That is God our Father's business!

THE BISHOP

That is His business! Yes, that is the right expression! Thank you, my venerable friend!

BLANK

I mean, that miracles are subject to just as strict a conformity to law as everything else, although we cannot perceive the law. I mean the same as Professor Petersen means.

FALK

In that book, which he never publishes?

BLANK

But which he purposes to publish in the course of a few years.

Then, if that be so, —— what weight attaches to the particular miracle,——whether we shortsighted mortals can discern such a law or not?

If our flocks believe that they see it, then let us praise God with them.

THE BISHOP

Then you mean that we ought to give our sanction to the miracle?

BLANK

Neither to give our sanction nor to refuse it. We should simply praise God along with our flocks.

THE BISHOP

No, my venerable friend, we shall not get out of the difficulty with praise.

THE CLERGY

[*Muttering among themselves.*] We shall not get out of this difficulty with praise. No, we shall not get out of this difficulty with praise.

THE BISHOP

Herr Brej will speak.

BREJ

I really cannot understand what there can be to hinder us from immediately sanctioning the miracle. Is it then so rare a thing? I am *always* seeing miracles. We are so accustomed to them in my parish, that the wonder would be *not* to see them.

F

FALK

Could not Brej be so kind as to tell us something about those miracles in his parish at home?

THE BISHOP

No, or we shall wander from the point.——
You have risen, Herr Jensen; do you wish to speak?

JENSEN

Yes. Everything depends in this case on the fact which confronts us. Is it a miracle, ——perhaps several—— ; or is it not a miracle?

KRÖJER

Just so.

JENSEN

Each separate miracle must be investigated. But then we must have a technical opinion, a good medical opinion, and possibly sworn evidence taken before a clever lawyer. Given all this,——then only can the clergy with safety deliver their spiritual opinion.

By 'spiritual' I do not mean what we see and hear here of lay-preachers and other so-called godly or inspired persons.

I mean in this instance, as elsewhere, a plain, solid, dry fact,——all the more spiritual; the plainer, the solider, and the drier it is.

FALK

Hear, hear!

JENSEN

Perhaps in this way it might be demonstrated that a miracle never comes like this. Never!

It does not come expected, courted by hundreds, may be thousands, in excitement and curiosity.

Yes, curiosity!

No, when a miracle comes it is a real, dry, quiet, plain fact, for real, dry, quiet, plain people.

FALK

That is out of my own heart.

KRÖJER

If Falk will allow me, I should just like to make a remark. Since I came up here as pastor, I have observed that the driest men are often those that most easily fall a prey to superstition.

BLANK

Very true! That is precisely my experience!

KRÖJER

They often deny out of mere disbelief what is manifest to all eyes. But then they are, so to speak, assailed by an unaccountable panic in the rear, and thereupon become convinced of things that are quite invisible to the rest of us.

I have often thought, that the supernatural has become an hereditary need in man to such a degree, that if we resist it in one way——

BLANK

——it comes out in another! I have thought so, myself.

FALK

Ah, whether it comes from the dry or the green, I really must ask if your meaning is, that we should give up now, whatever order and precision we have attained in the Church, and begin roving about again like ordained owls?

BREJ

Do you refer to me?
[*The Clergy roar with laughter.*

THE BISHOP

Hshshshshshsh.—— . . . Let us remember that there is a sick person within!

FALK

The craving for miracles is an excrescence on faith of the same sort as Lay ministration

on the Teaching Office,——a disorder, a
disease, in fact an atavism, an eructation.

[*The Clergy suppress their laughter and
consequently begin to cough.*

Hshshshshshsh !

The miracle which is not sanctioned by the
clergy, which is not so to speak assessed and
entered by the supreme ecclesiastical courts
under the presidence of His Majesty the King,
I regard as a vagrant, a vagabond, a house-
breaker.

[*The Bishop suppresses his laughter and the
Clergy do the same, keeping their eyes
on the Bishop.*

It may be a fine thing to be *naïf*. I too have
been *naïf*. But when a man is pastor in a
large town and must mourn with the mourners
over a grave at one o'clock,——and make
merry with a bridal party at three,——and
perhaps attend the deathbed of the poor at
four,——and dine at the Castle at five,——he
then learns to recognise the instability of man.
He then learns not to put his trust in persons
but rather in institutions.

Where the miracle appears, every institution founders in a storm of sensationalism !

The Catholic Church, therefore, has tried to organise the miracle as an institution. But it has thereby lost the regard of all intelligent men, and has nothing left to it but silly, self-seeking souls.

I was once in a company of ladies; there was only myself and about twenty of them. [*Mirth.*] One of these ladies was seized with the cramp. Immediately afterwards another. And then, one after another, until there were six. [*The mirth increases.*] So I took some cold water and threw it——first upon the six, one after another [*He imitates the action with his hand*]; and then on several of the others as well; for that sort of thing is infectious. [*Loud laughter.*

THE BISHOP

[*Recovers himself first.*] Hshshshshshsh ! [*Then he bursts out laughing again and the rest with him; he recovers himself:*] Hshshshshshsh !

FALK

I think that is sound. Throw cold water upon it !

[*Laughter and coughing in pocket handker-chiefs still continue. Some of the Clergy thank him cordially.*

KRÖJER

We know Falk, and know that he is a good man, —— in spite of his eccentricity. I think, if for instance he saw the old pastor's widow here——she is now nearly a hundred years old,——he would be the last person to throw cold water on her,——although she does go about amongst us, a living miracle, infecting us all with her faith. The same applies to the young girl, Aagaat Florvaagen, who takes care of the old lady. The miracle which awakened her, I saw myself, and many others with me. Before *our* eyes, under *our* hands, she lay dead and cold. And he prayed over her and took her by the hand and raised her up ! You must believe a man's testimony ! [*Astonishment.*
They are here now.

SEVERAL

They are here ?

KRÖJER

Perhaps they are coming into this room. They are coming straight towards this house, but it takes them a long time. The old lady wants to see. She wants to see her whom the landslip could not awaken.
I ask you to look at this old woman ! Talk

to her! Talk to the girl, who comes with her! You will receive answers as clear and trustworthy as her own face.

This will bring us further forward than all our *doctrinaire* explanations.

I do not say so for the sake of finding fault. I have myself thought as you do——even until I became a pastor up here. No one has felt more acutely than I felt formerly, what concessions the Church has been obliged to make here, and what paltry doctrines, what wretched evasions alone are left to us.

We are poor, without the power of working miracles,——without heart to pray for the power,——and must pretend, either that we can afford to despise it, or else that we possess it and are rich!

I know each one of you so far, that if you dared,——yes, if you were perfectly confident that you had seen here a miracle so great as to fulfil the immortal condition of the Bible : ' All they that saw it believed' :——ah, however feeble any of you may be otherwise, you would become even as little children, you would devote yourselves body and soul, you would give up all the days of your lives that are left to you, in order to preach it.

[*Emotion, especially among the elder Clergy.*

I may make these confessions on your behalf, my brethren, because I stand within

that circle of the Spirit, whereof it is written :
' Either within or without ! ' If a man is once
within, all the disguises of poverty fall of
themselves, and we have strength to confess
the truth !

What is there left of Christianity, if the
Church has now lost its miraculous power ?

ELIAS

[*Comes in from out of doors.*] Excuse me !
——Here is some one, who wishes to see my
mother. It is the old pastor's widow.

> [*They all stand up. Then they see at the
> door the pastor's widow and Aagaat. Elias
> opens the door, which leads in to the right,
> and goes in himself. The Clergy have moved
> their chairs and draw back respectfully.*

THE PASTOR'S WIDOW

> [*Who has come in as far as the threshold of
> the middle room.*

Leave me now, Aagaat !——Now I desire
to be alone.——Alone.——For here, where
the Lord has been,——is holy ground.——
This is holy ground.——Here it is ' face to
face.'——And here it is best to be alone.

> [*She stands where she can see into the bed-
> room. Then she bows herself. She
> stretches out both her hands into the air
> with great ecstasy. Then she looks in
> again, makes a reverence, and turns to go.*

She was white.——Shining white.——I thought she would be so.——Shining white. And slept like a child.——Now I have seen it.——Such a sight is a revelation.——Oh, what a revelation is here!——Thank you, for allowing me to be alone.

AAGAAT

But were you alone?

THE PASTOR'S WIDOW

Quite alone.——No one but I.——She was shining white.   [*They are now outside.*

ELIAS

[*Comes in from the right.*] Both the other doors are shut again. Now I will shut this.
          [*He goes out. The Clergy still stand silent.*

KRÖJER

You did not speak to her?

THE BISHOP

——No.

KRÖJER

There is a gleam of sunlight on all your faces.——I will tell you why:——men on whom the miraculous power has lightened, reflect the light.

Let us talk of this!
          [*They re-assemble and sit down again.*

JENSEN

May I ask a question? —— Do you not consider Conversion a miracle?

KRÖJER

What we call the miracle of Conversion, can be followed psychologically, step by step; therefore it is not a miracle.

It has its equivalent in other great religions and in purely moral conversion, although that goes on in secret.

But a Christianity, which is founded upon miracles and in process of time has lost the power to work them,——what is that?

Mere morality.

FALK

The essence of Christianity is not miracles; but faith in the Resurrection.

KRÖJER

——which all the great religions have? Which all men of religious feeling have?

FALK

——but without the childlike dependence.

KRÖJER

That is true. Without that.

FALK

Therefore also without the great self-sacrifice.

KRÖJER

No, there you are wrong!

The bearing of the martyr's cross,——did that come into the world first with Christianity? The boundless happiness of living and dying for what we love,——did we learn that from Christianity?

That was on earth before Christianity; it is on earth side by side with Christianity at this very time——in every conceivable form.

THE BISHOP

What then do you mean by Christianity?

KRÖJER

For me, Christianity is infinitely more than a moral system. We find other moral systems more fully and accurately expounded in other places than the New Testament. To me it is infinitely more than the power of self-sacrifice; or else there is much besides on a level with it.

Either Christianity is life in God, beyond the world and all its moralities; or it *is not*. Either it is more than devotion to any ideal whatsoever, that is to say——a new world, a miracle; or it *is not*.

[*He sits down trembling and exhausted.*

There was so much . . . I ought to have said ; . . . but . . . I cannot.

THE BISHOP

Directly you came on board to-day, dear Kröjer, I saw that you were ill and over-strained. But all become so who follow Pastor Sang !

THE STRANGER

[*Has opened the door from the veranda, and leaves it so. He has gradually approached.*
May I be allowed to speak.

[*They all turn round ; some rise.*

THE BISHOP

Brant, is that you ?

OTHERS

Pastor Brant ?

OTHERS

Is *that* Brant ?

THE BISHOP

You were not with us ? How did you come here ?

BRANT

Over the mountains.

THE BISHOP

Over the mountains ?——Then you are not on your way to the Mission ?

BRANT

No, hither.

THE BISHOP

I understand you.

BRANT

It is the miracle that I seek.——And so I came yesterday, just as the landslip fell. I stood on the mountain a little way off and saw it. And I heard the bell ring.——And I have been here since.——And this morning I saw a sick man carried to the church, and, at the sound of the pastor's psalm within, rise up, thank God, and go. May I have leave to speak?

THE BISHOP

Certainly.

BRANT

I am a man in need, come to beg you for help, my brothers.

THE BISHOP

Speak, my dear friend!

BRANT

I say to myself: 'Here I stand before the miracle at last';——and the next instant: 'Ah, but is it the miracle?'

For this is not the first place, I have come

to, seeking to see it. I have turned back disappointed from all the places in Europe famed for miracles. Here, indeed, faith is greater and simpler; and the man is great. What I have seen here has possessed me with supernatural force. And the next moment, comes doubt! You see, that is my curse! I have brought it upon myself, because for seven years, as a pastor, I promised a miracle to him that believes. I promised it to him, because so it was written,——although I myself doubted, for I had never seen one that believes do it! For seven years, I have preached what I did not believe.

For seven years, therefore, whenever the heavy days came (and they came often, and with them wakeful nights) have I also prayed fervently : 'Where is that miraculous power, which Thou didst promise to them that believe in Thee ?' [*He bursts into tears.*

THE BISHOP

Ah, *you* speak plainly ! You have always done that.

BRANT

He has said in binding words, each stronger than the last, that he that believes has this power. Yes, power to do greater things than the Son of Man did.

What has become of it, then ?

After eighteen hundred years of unbounded exercise of faith, is there still no one who believes so fully, as to be able to raise up a miracle amongst us ? Is God's own promise still unredeemed ?

The power of faith cannot have grown weaker. It cannot have fared with this faculty inversely to all the other faculties of the race, ——so that it has decreased by continual use. No !

After more than eighteen hundred years of preaching, in many, many races, it must form a heritage accumulated during a thousand years, multiplied by education.

And still it is not yet strong enough to yield a miracle ? All the longing of believers combined cannot yet produce one individual possessing that miraculous power which makes all them that see it believe ? For this condition of the Bible must be present ! The Bible says repeatedly : 'All they that saw it believed.'——Thus, a miracle that makes all those that see it believe !——And thousands on thousands fall away ; for in spite of the promise, it is not given.

Men of modern education, enlightened women of our times, do not trouble themselves with those things which men or women

formerly believed as a matter of course. Not
because their power of faith is less, but
because it is better assured. Their devotion
is of a so much deeper and intenser kind, that,
as is natural and even just, it is all the more
difficult to win. He who does win it, wins
the most that is still given in the world !

Therefore : stake the proportionate value !
Or else you will never win it.

[*Subdued talking among the Clergy.*

Religion is no longer man's only ideal. If
it is to be his highest, then you must prove
that it is so ! He can live and die for what
he loves,——for his country, his family, his
convictions. And since this is the highest
that can be found within the bounds of things
natural, and you must show him something
higher still, —— then, pass these bounds !
Show him the miraculous power !

[*Great agitation among the Clergy.*

FALK

[*Rises.*] There is somewhere written a
word of wrath concerning that generation
which will not believe unless it sees a sign.

BRANT

And do you know what that generation
answers ?

'We only ask for those signs which God

Himself has promised,——promised to him
that believes! Or have you not yet a single
believer amongst you?——What then will
you have us do?'

Yes, that is the answer of this generation.

But give this same generation a miracle,——
one that the sharpest instruments of scepticism
cannot dissect,——one of which it can be
said : 'All they that saw it, believed,'——then
you may yet live to realise that it is not the
power of faith which fails us ; but the miracle.

[*Agitation among the Clergy.*

There is no need for the teacher to put a
premium on credulity. The germs of faith
are the strongest and most numerous just in
the sharpest-witted sceptic! Is there any one
who knows civilised man and does not know
that? Is there any pastor who has not experienced, that in general the danger is just
the opposite : for want of the real they fall
into belief in the unreal.

SEVERAL

[*In an undertone.*] That is true.

BRANT

If a miracle appeared amongst us,——one so
great, that 'all they that saw it believed'——?

First the millions would come thronging to

it,——those who live in misery, longing for it, —— the disappointed, the oppressed, the suffering, those who look for Righteousness.

If they heard that the Kingdom of God in the old sense of the word had descended upon the earth again, . . . be it where it might,——in tears or rejoicing,——yes, if they knew that most of them were in jeopardy of dying on the way,——better die on that way than live on any other! They would crawl out each from his town, his cabin, his bed,——the sick before ——forth to the manifestation of God.

And they would not be alone. All that seek for truth upon the earth would follow after. First those whose need of truth is the strongest, the profound, earnest seekers, the exalted souls. Their fervour would be the noblest, their faith of most avail. It is not the longing for truth, not the power of faith which fails them, but the miracle!

All men desire peace and certainty on the greatest question in the world. Even the thoughtless, those who have laid it aside as useless or impossible! They are all, without exception, reared up to long for more than they know, that is to say, for faith. But give them the pledge——the pledge that the teaching is true! If they see that, then they will believe also what they do not see.

It was so from the first.

Those who now can be content with less,
——with their personal experience :——do
like Mahometans, Jews, and Buddhists. These
too all appeal to their personal experience !

The pledge that this personal experience is
general truth, that is what is lacking.

But that is what I seek ! For that is
promised !

O God, my God ! I stand here before my
last trial.

THE BISHOP

Brant, Brant !

BRANT

Before my last trial. For the struggle is
beyond my strength. I renounce my vocation,
——I renounce the Church, I renounce the
faith,——if, if, if——! [*He bursts into tears.*

THE BISHOP

My dear son ! You must not——

BRANT

No, do not talk to me !——I entreat you !
——No, help me to pray ! For if the miracle
is not here, then it cannot *be* ! This man is
certainly more than other men ; he is the
noblest that the earth bears ! Such faith as

his, no man has seen. Neither has any man seen such faith in his faith.

ALL

That is true !

BRANT

And is not that easy to understand ? When he came here he had great possessions. He has given it all. There is no reckoning how often he has risked his life in bringing help to others. There is no reckoning the miracles which they believe he has worked. Just because there were so many, I did not believe in them.

THE CLERGY

[*In an undertone.*] It was the same with me.

BRANT

But perhaps we ought strictly to have thought the opposite ? That *this* is what is meant by 'faith'? The very existence of faith is the working of miracles ! It must work miracles ! Perhaps we ought to have thought so ?

Whatever we ought to have thought, we ought not to have looked so professionally, so doubtfully upon him, as I, alas ! have done. His love and faith ought to have made me humble. I accuse myself and beg his forgiveness, from the bottom of my heart !

ALL THE CLERGY

[*Without exception.*]   And I too !   And I too !

BRANT

He is the best man we know ; he has the greatest faith, that now exists ;——What if the miracle were here ?   [*Emotion.*

JENSEN

[*Whispering.*]   Look at that cross over the door ?   Is it the evening sun——or what is it ?

BRANT

I do not know.   But be sure of this, that if the miracle appears, thousands that we may not see will be present at its appearing.

If only we could but be present !——If only we could but be present too.   Think ! to live to see anything so stupendous, that ' All they that saw it believed !'

Might we come to be witnesses of that,—— you——and you——and I ?   It is too much ; it cannot be possible !—— —— ——

But if it is possible,——then, my brethren, there are others living in this our time,—— Alas ! feeble, of little faith, uncharitable of that we are !——

ALL

——Yes, yes !—— ——

BRANT

——*Others,* our brethren, not so highly favoured as we; for it is *we,* the unworthy, that are called ! [*Deep emotion.*] And when I look out upon this naked region lying here, imprisoned, under the cry of the seamews, on the brink of the fjord, and when I think how the Kingdom of God began in rich and fertile meadows by the side of the great highway in the land of the Sun,——what a witness would it be, if it were renewed in all its greatness here, in a poor, distant hamlet, nigh to eternal ice—— —— ——

FALK

[*Rises deathly pale and whispers :*] Yes, yes !

SEVERAL

Yes, yes !

BRANT

——then it seems to me, all things work together, and the miracle may come !

[*They have all risen.*

THE BISHOP

[*Softly.*] Oh, if it might come, so that I might see it, before I die !

BLANK

Yes, if we were but taken up in this great faith !

Not because we deserve to see ; but because we need it.

[*The old man falls upon his knees ; and then immediately several others.*

BRANT

Because the whole generation needs it ! More and more, each time. Because it is promised. Because it must be here if it *is*.

[*He kneels down.*

His faith must be able to reach it ! His is the greatest on the earth ! And faith is able ! It is able indeed.

ALL

It is able, it is able !

BRANT

——If it were not,——then it would all be impossible.

Then the rest would not be true either. Then there would be something boundless in all this . . . !

Something beyond us . . . !

The Fifth Scene

RAKEL

[*Is heard within calling in terror.*]   Elias !
  [*She comes rushing in from the right, straight
    towards the window, which she opens, call-
    ing out with all her might :*
Elias !
  [*Then she throws herself back, and would fall
    if Kröjer did not catch her.   She bursts
    into tears, but immediately rises in terror,
    and points into her mother's room.*
There ! There ! She is no longer alone !
——*Look,*——look !   [*They have all risen.*
  [*Elias appears at the same moment in the
    veranda.   Rakel immediately tears herself
    away and rushes towards him :*
Mother ! Mother !

ELIAS

Has she risen up ?

RAKEL

Yes, yes !

ELIAS

And walks ?

RAKEL

Yes !——but she is not alone !

ELIAS

That must be proclaimed !

RAKEL

Not to father !

ELIAS

No, on the housetop, in the belfry, ringing out over the whole world !   [*He is gone.*

RAKEL

But you have no ladder?   [*She gets no answer; in terror:*] But there is no ladder !

KRÖJER

[*With a motion of the hand, softly.*]   Hush !

THE BISHOP

[*Whispering.*]   Ah ! listen !

> [*They all hear coming from the church :*
> Hallelujah, hallelujah !
> Hallelujah, hallelujah !

ALL

[*Fall on their knees, whispering.*]   He knows it !   He knows it !

> [*Then comes in Klara walking slowly in her white linen. Her eyes are fixed upon the church; she stands still and stretches out her hands towards the singing.*

ALL THE CLERGY [*answer in low chorus*]

> Hallelujah ! hallelujah !
> Hallelujah ! hallelujah !

RAKEL

[*In the balcony.*] Father stands at the door.
[*We hear him now singing, in a strong, clear voice :*

> Hallelujah ! hallelujah !
> Hallelujah ! hallelujah !

[*Then the church bell and all the people join in. There is such a storm of rejoicing, that it sounds as if thousands were singing. It is increased by the people hurrying up from among the trees. There is a moment when it seems as if these 'Hallelujahs' would lift the house from its foundations.*

Sang appears in the doorway; the evening sun falls upon his face. All rise and draw back.

He stretches out both his arms to Klara, who stands in the middle of the room. She stretches out her arms to him; he goes to her and embraces her. The singing surges round them. The room and the veranda are full of people; they press upon each other; others stand in the window.

Then she sinks slowly down on his shoulder.

*The singing ceases ; the church bell sounds
alone.*

*She makes an effort to gather her strength and
rise. She succeeds partially, then she raises her
head and looks at him.*]

KLARA

Ah, thou wert glorious, . . . when thou
didst come to me, . . . O my beloved !
　　[*Her head droops again, her arms fall, and
　　her whole body sinks down.*

SANG

　　[*Stands and holds her ; he lays his hand
　　on her heart ; then he bends over her, in
　　astonishment. He looks up to heaven, and
　　says in a childlike way :*
But this was not the meaning ?——
　　[*He bends one knee and lays her head upon
　　it ; he looks at her more closely, lays her
　　down tenderly and stands up ; then he looks
　　upwards again :*
But this was not the meaning——? Or
else—— ?—— —— Or else——?
　　　　[*He clutches at his heart ; and falls.*
　　[*Rakel has stood petrified, looking on. She
　　now gives a loud scream, and falls on her
　　knees by her parents.*

KRÖJER

What did he mean——'Or else——?' what?

BRANT

I do not know for certain.——But he is dead because of it.

RAKEL

Dead?——Impossible ! [*The bell tolls on.*

The Reader is referred to—

Leçons sur le système nerveux : faites par J. M. Charcot : recueillies et publiées par le Dr. Bourneville. 3ᵉ édition. 2 vols. Paris, 1881. Chez A. Delahaye et E. Lecrosnier.

Études cliniques sur l'hystéro-épilepsie ou grande hystérie : par le Dr. Richer. 1 vol. Paris, 1881. Chez A. Delahaye et E. Lecrosnier.

NOTE.—The above are the Author's references.

W. W.